ABIODUN THORPE

Beneath Amulet Chronicles

Secrets of Ava's Ixchel Adventure

Copyright © 2024 by Abiodun Thorpe

All rights reserved. No part of this publication may be reproduced, stored or transmitted in any form or by any means, electronic, mechanical, photocopying, recording, scanning, or otherwise without written permission from the publisher. It is illegal to copy this book, post it to a website, or distribute it by any other means without permission.

This novel is entirely a work of fiction. The names, characters and incidents portrayed in it are the work of the author's imagination. Any resemblance to actual persons, living or dead, events or localities is entirely coincidental.

First edition

This book was professionally typeset on Reedsy. Find out more at reedsy.com

Contents

Introduction	1
1 Chapter One: The Shadow of the Past	2
Ava Whitmore: A Life of Independence and Loss	2
Damian Cross: The Mercenary Seeking Redemption	4
Back to the Present: The Peru Chase	7
2 Chapter Two: Into the Depths	10
A Shift in the Shadows, Tentative Alliance	15
Temple Clues and Confessions	18
3 Chapter Three: The Secrets Beneath	21
Unveiling the Truth in the Temple	21
The Betrayal and Rescue	27
4 Chapter Four: Desires and Deception	29
Seduction Under the Stars	29
An Unexpected Ally	31
The Path to the Key	35
A Twist of Betrayal	36
5 Chapter Five: Shadows of the Past	37
The Aftermath of Betrayal	37
A Reluctant Alliance	39
The Stronghold and the Seduction	41
Confronting Elena and Elliot	42
A Fight for Legacy	45
Obsession and Redemption	46

6	Chapter Six: Whispers in the Shadows	48
	A New Ally?	50
	Marisol's Connection	51
7	Chapter Seven: Echoes of the Past	57
	Trial By Shadows	59
	Ava's Infiltration of the Mercenary Camp	61
	Tying to the Elder's Words	62
8	Chapter Eight: Beneath Amulet Chronicles	64
	The Elliot's Insinuations	66
	Elliot and Elena's Fates	69
9	Conclusion	71
About the Author		73

Introduction

Beneath the Amulet Chronicles: Secrets of Ava's Ixchel Adventure takes readers on an electrifying journey through the dense, mysterious jungles of Peru. With every page, the story delves deeper into the secrets of the Amulet of Ixchel, a relic shrouded in myth, power, and danger. Ava Whitmore, an intrepid archaeologist chasing both answers and redemption, is thrust into a treacherous game of survival. Beside her is Damian Cross, a brooding mercenary whose haunted past collides with her own desperate quest. Their journey is one of fierce determination, sizzling chemistry, and a shared fight against ruthless enemies and their inner demons. As they unravel the amulet's riddles, they uncover truths that test the limits of trust, love, and legacy. This is a tale of passion, betrayal, and adventure that grips readers and doesn't let go.

1

Chapter One: The Shadow of the Past

Ava Whitmore: A Life of Independence and Loss

Ava Whitmore was forged by tragedy. Her father's abandonment and her mother's mysterious death drove her to build a life of self-reliance and intellectual pursuit. Her career in archaeology became her sanctuary, an escape from the emotional chaos of her past. Yet, when a letter from her estranged father leads her to Peru, it stirs unresolved grief and a gnawing need for answers. The Amulet of Ixchel becomes more than an artifact—it's a key to understanding the man who left her life in ruins. As Ava searched through the abandoned cabin, she stumbled upon a weathered leather journal tucked beneath a loose floorboard. The pages were filled with her father's frantic scrawl, sketches of ancient symbols, and fragmented notes. "The key is not what it seems," one entry read. "Its power can heal or destroy—but only in the right hands."

Ava's breath hitched as she recognized a sketch of the amulet.

CHAPTER ONE: THE SHADOW OF THE PAST

Her father had been so close, yet so far. She clutched the journal tightly, determination burning in her chest. "We're going to finish this," she whispered.

This discovery connects Ava more deeply to her father's journey and provides critical insights for the story's progression.

Ava had arrived in Peru three days earlier, chasing a trail that started with a letter postmarked from an untraceable location. Her father's handwriting had been unmistakable, and the single sheet of paper had contained two things: a fragment of an ancient map and a warning to trust no one. Trust had never come easily to Ava—not since her father had walked out on her and her mother when she was fifteen, leaving a trail of broken promises and unanswered questions in his wake.

Her mother's disappearance two years later had been the final fracture in her family. Official reports called it a tragic accident— a fall during a late-night hike—but Ava had always felt there was more to the story. Without her father to turn to and with no family to guide her, Ava became fiercely independent. She buried herself in books, determined to find stability in the chaos of her life.

After earning her degree in archaeology, Ava had buried herself in her work, her reputation built on unraveling ancient puzzles and finding meaning in forgotten relics. She'd told herself she didn't care about the man who'd abandoned her, but the moment she saw that letter, something inside her cracked. The amulet wasn't just another artifact; it was a chance to piece together the fragments of her family and uncover the truth her father had hidden from her.

But Ava was no stranger to danger. She'd spent years navigating treacherous digs, fending off rivals, and learning how to protect herself. The blade strapped to her thigh wasn't for show—it was a necessity.

Damian Cross: The Mercenary Seeking Redemption

Damian Cross lives in a shadow of guilt, his mercenary past marked by betrayals and choices he can't undo. His latest assignment is clear-cut: retrieve the amulet for a shadowy collector. But when he sees Ava in the chaotic streets of a Peruvian market, something about her ignites his protective instincts. Damian is a man of contradictions—cunning and hardened but with a flicker of conscience. Meeting Ava disrupts his solitary path, forcing him to confront a world where trust might be more powerful than strategy.

Damian had arrived in Peru under vastly different circumstances. He was a mercenary by trade, a man who thrived on adrenaline and the kind of jobs most people wouldn't touch with a ten-foot pole. His past was a blur of questionable choices and burned bridges, but he carried it all with a casual confidence that belied the guilt he kept buried deep. Damian's childhood had been a relentless struggle. Raised in the shadow of an abusive father and a mother too scared to leave, Damian learned early how to fight and how to survive. At sixteen, he ran away, leaving behind a world of violence and despair. But the ghosts of his past followed him, driving him toward dangerous jobs and risk-filled work. Redemption, for Damian, wasn't just a word—it was a distant hope that someday his choices might outweigh his sins.

This job wasn't supposed to be personal. He'd been hired by a shadowy collector to retrieve the Amulet of Ixchel—a job that promised a payday big enough to wipe his slate clean. No more debts, no more ghosts from the past chasing him in the dark. But Damian wasn't a thief or a thug, not entirely. He had rules. He didn't hurt innocent people, and he didn't make promises he couldn't keep. That didn't mean he didn't know how to play dirty when the situation called for it.

He'd first spotted Ava at the market, her fiery hair a beacon against the muted colors of the crowd. She didn't fit the mold of the usual treasure hunters—too refined, too focused, and far too reckless to survive long in this world. She intrigued him, and when he saw the men tailing her, he made a split-second decision to intervene. Maybe it was curiosity, or maybe it was the way she held herself, defiant and unyielding despite the odds stacked against her. Whatever the reason, he couldn't just walk away.

The humid air of Cusco, Peru, clung to Ava Whitmore's skin, its oppressive weight matching the tightness in her chest. It was 2:15 PM, and the bustling San Pedro Market was alive with a chaotic symphony of voices in Spanish and Quechua. Vendors hawked colorful tapestries and sizzling street food, their calls blending with the rhythmic sounds of traditional Andean music echoing from the nearby Plaza de Armas. This place had been a cradle of history, with every corner hinting at stories untold. The ancient ruins of Sacsayhuamán loomed nearby, a testament to the Inca Empire's once-unmatched engineering, now shadowed by her pursuit of the Amulet of Ixchel. She adjusted the strap of her satchel and glanced over her shoulder, her instincts prickling. The crowded streets of the market were a kaleidoscope of sound and movement, but something felt wrong. The buzz of conversations in Spanish and Quechua, the smells of sizzling meats and ripe fruit, the persistent cries of vendors hawking their wares—all of it dulled under the sharp edge of her unease.

She wasn't alone.

Ava quickened her pace, ducking past a stall selling handwoven tapestries, her eyes scanning for a way out. The satchel pressed against her hip held something worth dying for—or killing for. The map fragment was her first solid lead to the Amulet of Ixchel, an artifact wrapped in myth and power, something her estranged father had been chasing before his mysterious disappearance. She'd been searching for years, not for treasure but for answers. Now, standing at the precipice of discovery, she felt the weight of every decision that had led her here.

A voice—low, smooth, and laced with danger—broke through her thoughts. "You're not very subtle, are you?"

Ava spun, her knife already in her hand. The man standing before her was tall and broad-shouldered, his dark hair tousled in a way that suggested he hadn't brushed it but somehow made it look intentional. His clothes—worn leather jacket, faded jeans, and boots caked in dirt—marked him as someone who thrived on danger. But it was his eyes, a sharp steel-gray, that sent a shiver down her spine.

"And who the hell are you?" she demanded, knife still raised.

The man raised his hands in mock surrender, a crooked smile tugging at his lips. "Name's Damian Cross. You can put the knife down unless you're planning to use it."

She didn't lower it. "Why are you following me?"

Damian's smile widened. "Me? Following you? Hate to break

it to you, sweetheart, but you're not the only one after the map."

Her stomach twisted. How much did this stranger know? And worse, who else was involved?

Before she could respond, a commotion erupted behind her. A group of men, clearly armed and not subtle about it, pushed through the market crowd. Ava didn't need to guess who they were after.

"Friends of yours?" Damian asked, his tone light but his stance shifting into something sharper, more predatory.

"Not likely," Ava snapped.

"Well, then," he said, stepping closer. "How about we get out of here, and you can tell me why half the underworld is chasing you?"

Ava hesitated for a fraction of a second before the men spotted her. One of them shouted, pointing in her direction. She cursed under her breath.

"Fine," she bit out. "But if you're lying to me, I'll make you regret it."

Damian's grin was maddening. "Wouldn't dream of it."

Back to the Present: The Peru Chase

Peru is a land where history bleeds through the surface of every stone. The humid air carries the scent of earth and mystery, and the dense jungle conceals ancient ruins steeped in myth. The market where Ava first encounters danger is a vibrant tapestry of culture, with stalls brimming with colorful tapestries, sizzling street food, and relics of lost civilizations. Beyond the market lies a world of archeological wonder—hidden temples etched with cryptic carvings, treacherous caverns guarded by ancient traps, and lush landscapes that pulse with life and danger. Ava and Damian darted through the market, weaving between stalls and dodging startled vendors. The men pursuing them were gaining ground, their shouts growing louder. Damian led the way, his movements quick and calculated, while Ava stayed close, her knife still gripped tightly in her hand.

"This way," Damian called, veering into a narrow alley.

They emerged into a quieter street, the noise of the market fading behind them. Damian stopped abruptly, turning to face her.

"Nice moves back there," he said, his tone almost approving. "Where'd you learn to handle a blade like that?"

"None of your business," Ava shot back, her chest heaving as she tried to catch her breath. "Why are you helping me?"

Damian's grin returned, lazy and infuriating. "Let's just say I have a soft spot for fiery redheads with a knack for trouble."

Ava glared at him. "You're enjoying this, aren't you?"

"Immensely," he admitted. "But you might want to save the interrogation for later. Something tells me this isn't over."

He wasn't wrong. The faint sound of footsteps echoed in the distance, drawing closer. Ava squared her shoulders, her instincts screaming at her to run. But she didn't.

"Let's make a deal," Damian said, his voice dropping to a serious tone. "You've got the map. I've got the skills to keep us both alive. Work with me, and we might just have a shot at finding this thing."

Ava hesitated, every fiber of her being screaming not to trust him. But trust wasn't a luxury she could afford right now.

"Fine," she said through gritted teeth. "But if you double-cross me—"

"I won't," Damian said, his gaze steady. "Not unless you give me a reason to."

Damian crouched by the fire, staring into the flickering flames. Ava could see the weight he carried etched in the tightness of his jaw. "There was a girl," he began, his voice rough with the strain of old wounds. "She trusted me, and I failed her. I walked away, thinking it would keep her safe, but the people after me... they didn't care. They found her anyway."

Ava sat silently, the confession hanging heavy between them. "Is that why you're here now?" she asked softly. Damian nodded, his steel-gray eyes meeting hers. "If I can stop Elliot—stop anyone from wielding the amulet—maybe I can make up for some of it."

This deepens Damian's motivations, tying his quest to a personal redemption arc and giving his actions more weight.

The challenge hung between them, unspoken but electric. Ava didn't trust him, but as they disappeared into the jungle together, she couldn't shake the feeling that Damian Cross might be the only person who could keep her alive.

2

Chapter Two: Into the Depths

The jungle wasn't just alive—it was ancient, a living testament to the passage of civilizations long forgotten. Massive ceiba trees towered overhead, their roots tangling like ancient veins through the damp earth. Birds with brilliant plumage flitted through the canopy, their calls echoing like a natural symphony. Every so often, Ava would catch a glimpse of something carved into the rocks—a spiral, a figure, or a symbol—that hinted at the jungle's hidden past.

"This place is older than the Inca," she mused aloud, her voice breaking the steady rhythm of their footsteps. "The amulet's story could predate even the gods they worshiped."

Damian glanced back at her, his machete resting on his shoulder. "All the more reason to keep moving. Legends don't mean much if we don't make it out alive." Every step was accompanied by the symphony of rustling leaves, chirping insects, and the occasional distant howl that sent shivers racing

CHAPTER TWO: INTO THE DEPTHS

down Ava's spine. The air, thick with humidity, clung to her skin like a second layer, and every breath tasted of earth and decay.

In a remote village, Ava and Damian met an elder shaman who spoke of Ixchel's wrath and mercy. "The amulet's power," the shaman intoned, "is tied to balance. Its bearer must prove their worth by facing their greatest fear. Fail, and the amulet will consume you."

The shaman handed Ava a small carved totem. "This will guide you to the temple," he said. "But beware—the jungle guards its secrets fiercely." This adds richness to the lore and raises the stakes for Ava's quest.

The shaman's gaze was piercing, his voice heavy with the weight of ancient knowledge. "Ixchel, the goddess of creation and destruction, gave the amulet its power. But power demands sacrifice. Blood rituals were performed to ensure balance—life for life, strength for strength."

Ava shivered, her fingers brushing against the carved totem the shaman had given her. "So, the amulet requires blood?"

The shaman nodded solemnly. "Not just any blood. It must come from the bearer's greatest fear, their deepest weakness. Only then can the amulet's power be wielded without corruption. Fail, and the amulet will consume not only the bearer but everything around them."

The words lingered in the air like a dark omen. Damian's jaw tightened, his expression grim. "Sounds like a fairytale turned nightmare."

Ava wasn't so sure. Her father's disappearance, the cryptic warnings in his letter—it all pointed to the amulet's price being real.

Damian moved ahead, his pace unrelenting and confident, his machete flashing in the muted light as he cut through the dense vegetation. Ava followed closely, her mind racing as she replayed the events of the market. The men who had pursued them weren't ordinary thugs; their coordination and determination suggested something far more sinister.

"How much farther?" Ava asked, breaking the silence.

Damian glanced over his shoulder, his gray eyes gleaming with something between amusement and caution. "Not far. There's a clearing up ahead where we can set up camp."

"Camp?" She didn't bother masking her disbelief.

"Yes, camp," he said, stepping over a massive root that jutted out like a serpent coiled to strike. "Unless you'd prefer to keep going in the dark and stumble into quicksand or, I don't know, a jaguar's dinner plans."

Ava bit back a retort. She hated that he was right, but she hated more that he seemed to enjoy her discomfort. Still, the thought of resting, even briefly, was tempting. Her legs ached, and the weight of the satchel felt heavier with each passing hour.

Damian's pragmatic survival skills clashed with Ava's calculated precision. He moved through the jungle like a predator, confident and instinct-driven, while Ava analyzed every step, her mind racing to anticipate the unknown. He wielded his machete with an almost careless efficiency, cutting through dense vegetation, while she cringed at the damage to the fragile ecosystem.

"You hack at everything like it's an enemy," Ava muttered, watching him slice through a stubborn vine.

Damian chuckled, his voice tinged with amusement. "And you overthink everything like it's a math problem. Sometimes

CHAPTER TWO: INTO THE DEPTHS

you just have to cut through the noise, Red."

Ava frowned but said nothing, her scientific sensibilities clashing with Damian's brute practicality. They couldn't have been more different, yet somehow their strengths complemented each other in ways neither was ready to admit.

They reached the clearing just as the sun began its descent, the golden light painting the leaves in hues of amber and emerald. Damian worked quickly, gathering wood for a fire while Ava scouted the perimeter. Her knife stayed in her hand, her fingers brushing the familiar hilt as she scanned the shadows for any sign of movement.

"Relax," Damian called, his voice cutting through the quiet. "I didn't see any tracks nearby. We're safe for now."

Ava shot him a glare but said nothing. She didn't trust easily, and Damian's flippant confidence did little to ease her nerves.

As night fell, the fire crackled to life, casting flickering light across the clearing. Ava sat cross-legged, her satchel clutched protectively in her lap, while Damian lounged on the opposite side, the firelight accentuating the sharp lines of his face.

"So," he said, breaking the silence, "are you going to tell me why the map is so important, or are we playing the strong, silent type all night?"

Ava hesitated. Sharing the truth felt like giving him leverage, but keeping him in the dark could be just as dangerous. She settled for a half-truth.

"It's not the map itself," she said, her gaze fixed on the flames. "It's what it leads to."

Damian tilted his head, intrigued. "The Amulet of Ixchel."

Her eyes snapped to his, the fire reflected in their depths. "You know about it?"

"Of course I do," he said, a smirk tugging at his lips. "Legendary artifact, said to grant its bearer power over life and death. Every treasure hunter and black-market collector in the world has heard of it."

"It's not about the power," Ava said, her voice sharp. "It's about the truth."

Damian leaned forward, his interest piqued. "The truth about what?"

Ava hesitated, her fingers tightening around the satchel. She'd never spoken about her father to anyone—not since the day he'd vanished. But something about Damian's steady gaze, the quiet intensity that lingered behind his cocky facade, made her want to take the risk.

"My father," she said finally, the words tasting foreign on her tongue. "He was searching for the amulet before he disappeared. I need to know why."

Damian's expression shifted, a flicker of something—sympathy, perhaps—crossing his features. But it was gone as quickly as it had appeared.

"Fair enough," he said, leaning back. "But if you think this is just about family drama, you're wrong. The people chasing you aren't just after treasure. They'll kill for that map—and for the amulet."

"I'm aware," Ava said, her voice cold. "But I'm not walking away."

"Didn't think you would," Damian said, his smirk returning. "Stubbornness looks good on you."

Ava ignored the comment, turning her attention to the fire.

CHAPTER TWO: INTO THE DEPTHS

A Shift in the Shadows, Tentative Alliance

The jungle seemed to hold its breath as the night deepened. Ava stirred awake, the faint rustle of leaves dragging her from the edges of sleep. Her hand went instinctively to her knife as she scanned the darkness.

Damian was already awake, his machete in hand as he crouched near the edge of the clearing. He met her gaze, a silent warning in his eyes.

They weren't alone.

A shadow shifted in the trees, too deliberate to be the wind. Then came the sound—a low, guttural growl that sent a chill racing down Ava's spine.

"Jaguars don't usually hunt in groups," Damian whispered, his voice low but steady.

"That's comforting," Ava muttered, rising to her feet.

The first attacker lunged from the shadows, not an animal but a man cloaked in dark fabric, his face obscured. Ava ducked, her knife slicing through the air as Damian countered a second assailant. The clearing erupted into chaos, the firelight dancing wildly as blades clashed and bodies collided.

Ava's movements were quick and precise, her years of training taking over as she fought. But the attackers were skilled, their strikes calculated, their intent clear—they wanted the map.

"Run!" Damian shouted, his voice cutting through the melee.

"I'm not leaving you!" Ava yelled back, her blade catching the arm of an attacker who crumpled with a groan.

"No time for heroics, Red!" Damian growled, throwing one man into the fire before grabbing her arm.

Together, they bolted into the jungle, the cries of their pursuers fading behind them as the night swallowed them whole.

They didn't stop until they reached a rocky outcrop overlooking a river, the moonlight casting silver streaks across the rushing water. Ava leaned against a boulder, her chest heaving as she caught her breath. Damian stood nearby, his shirt torn and blood staining his knuckles.

"Still think you don't need my help?" he asked, his voice tinged with both exhaustion and amusement.

Ava glared at him but didn't argue. She hated to admit it, but without Damian, she might not have made it out alive.

"Fine," she said reluctantly. "But if we're doing this, we do it my way."

Damian grinned, his teeth flashing in the moonlight. "Wouldn't dream of it any other way, sweetheart."

As the adrenaline ebbed, Ava's body felt the full weight of the night's chaos. She sank onto a smooth rock, cradling the satchel against her side as Damian knelt by the river, splashing water on his face. The moon hung high above them, its silvery light illuminating the cuts and bruises they'd both earned in the fight.

"Who were they?" Ava asked, breaking the silence.

Damian ran a hand through his dark hair, his expression grim. "Could be anyone. Mercenaries, hired guns, rival treasure hunters. The amulet's got enough legends around it to draw the worst kinds of people."

Ava studied him, her skepticism returning. "And you're not one of them?"

He met her gaze, his gray eyes hard. "I've done things I'm not proud of, but I don't kill for sport or greed. If I wanted that map, I'd have taken it back in the clearing."

She hated that he made sense. "Then why are you here? What's in it for you?"

Damian stood, drying his hands on his jeans. "Call it redemption," he said, his tone lighter than the weight of his words. "Or maybe I just can't resist a good mystery."

"Right," Ava said, unimpressed. "You're just a mercenary with a heart of gold."

"I never said gold," he replied, his smirk reappearing.

The tension between them hung thick in the air, a precarious balance of mistrust and reliance. Damian moved closer, his gaze flicking to the satchel. "You didn't answer my question earlier," he said. "Why the map? Why the amulet? You mentioned your father, but there's more to this, isn't there?"

Ava's fingers tightened around the strap of the bag. She had spent years building walls around her emotions, guarding her motivations like a fortress. But in that moment, something cracked.

"My father believed the amulet could fix what was broken," she admitted, her voice soft. "Not just in the world but in people. He thought it could heal, restore, even bring back what was lost."

Damian frowned, his expression skeptical. "You believe that?"

"I don't know what I believe," she said. "But I know he gave everything to find it. And if I can understand why—if I can find it—it might give me the answers I've been chasing my whole life."

Damian let out a low whistle. "Heavy stuff, Red. You're not just chasing history; you're chasing ghosts."

"Don't call me Red," she snapped, though there was no real heat in her voice.

The corner of Damian's mouth lifted in a smile. "Fair enough. But you should know—whatever your reasons, there are people out there who'll kill to make sure you don't succeed."

"Then it's a good thing I have a mercenary watching my back," she said, standing and brushing dirt from her pants.

"You're learning," Damian said, grabbing his pack.

They exchanged a glance, something unspoken passing between them. Ava still didn't trust him, not entirely, but she couldn't deny that Damian was proving himself useful. And maybe—just maybe—he wasn't the villain she'd first assumed.

Temple Clues and Confessions

The dawn brought little relief from the oppressive heat of the jungle, but the golden light filtering through the trees cast the landscape in an ethereal glow. They trudged onward, following the faint markings on Ava's map fragment that hinted at a hidden temple deep within the jungle.

As they walked, Damian kept the conversation alive, his voice a mix of curiosity and humor.

"So, let me guess," he said, sidestepping a patch of mud. "You were the top of your class, the kind of student who made the professors swoon with your essays on ancient civilizations."

Ava rolled her eyes. "I worked hard because I had to. Nobody handed me anything on a silver platter."

"Not even your father?"

Her jaw tightened. "Especially not him."

Damian's smirk faded, his expression turning thoughtful. "You know, not all dads are meant to be heroes."

"What would you know about it?" Ava shot back, her tone

CHAPTER TWO: INTO THE DEPTHS

sharper than she intended.

"I know more than you think," he said, his voice quiet. "Let's just say I've had my fair share of disappointments too."

Ava glanced at him, surprised by the rawness in his tone. For all his bravado, there was a vulnerability in Damian that she hadn't expected.

Before she could respond, the jungle shifted again, the dense foliage giving way to a rocky incline. At the top, partially obscured by vines, was a stone structure etched with ancient symbols.

"The temple," Ava breathed, her exhaustion forgotten as excitement surged through her.

Damian whistled low, his eyes scanning the carvings. "Looks like we found your ghost's playground."

The entrance was narrow, the air inside cool and heavy with the scent of moss and damp stone. Ava held a flashlight, the beam cutting through the darkness as they descended a staircase carved into the rock. Damian followed, his machete at the ready.

The corridor opened into a vast chamber, its walls lined with intricate carvings depicting gods and rituals. At the center stood an altar, and atop it, a pedestal that seemed designed to hold something—something missing.

"This is it," Ava said, her voice barely a whisper. "This is where the amulet should be."

"But it's not," Damian noted, his gaze sweeping the room. "Which means someone got here first."

Ava's heart sank. She'd been so close, and now the trail seemed to end. But as she moved closer to the pedestal, she noticed something—a series of markings etched into the stone, almost like a code.

"What is it?" Damian asked, stepping beside her.

"Another clue," Ava said, her fingers brushing the carvings. "The amulet wasn't taken. It was moved."

"To where?"

Ava met his gaze, determination burning in her eyes. "We're about to find out."

Damian grinned, his earlier weariness replaced by excitement. "Well, Red - calling her by the nickname again, looks like the adventure's just getting started."

She didn't correct him this time as Damian's grin widened, Ava caught herself smiling despite the ache in her legs and the overwhelming exhaustion that weighed on her. She hated his cocky attitude, his constant teasing, but there was something disarming about the way he faced every danger with an easy charm.

For the first time, she didn't feel the need to argue or assert her independence. She was tired of fighting every moment, tired of carrying the weight of her father's legacy alone.

When he called her "Red" again, she didn't correct him. Instead, she let the nickname hang in the air, a small concession that felt strangely significant.

"Let's see where this leads," she said, her voice softer than before.

Damian's grin softened into something genuine. "Now you're talking."

The unspoken truce between them felt fragile, but it was a step forward. Together, they turned their attention to the markings, the promise of answers driving them onward into the unknown.

3

Chapter Three: The Secrets Beneath

Unveiling the Truth in the Temple

The air grew heavier as Ava and Damian descended deeper into the temple, the damp stone walls adorned with faint traces of painted glyphs long eroded by time. The flickering torchlight cast eerie shadows, bringing the carvings to life as if the figures were watching. The narrow corridor opened into a cavernous chamber, the ceiling soaring above them, lost in darkness. A faint metallic scent hung in the air, mingling with the smell of damp earth—a lingering echo of rituals performed centuries ago.

The carvings on the walls told a harrowing tale. Figures knelt in submission before a towering deity, their outstretched hands offering vessels of blood. Around them, jagged lines of fire and chaos radiated, a warning etched into stone for those who dared to wield the amulet's power. Ava shivered, the weight of history pressing down on her. Faint torchlight danced on the walls, revealing carvings that depicted vivid and violent scenes—a blood ritual where sacrifices empowered a mysterious figure holding the Amulet of Ixchel. Ava ran her fingers over the etchings, her mind racing with connections.

"These murals," she murmured, her voice hushed with awe, "they're telling a story—a warning." Her gaze snapped to Damian, who crouched beside an inscription. "Can you read it, this is incredible" Ava murmured, her fingers tracing the jagged lines etched into the wall. Her mind raced to piece together the symbolism, searching for connections in the mythology. "It's not just a ritual—it's a covenant. A warning against imbalance."

Damian leaned against a nearby column, his eyes scanning the room with practiced precision. "Looks more like a massacre to me," he said bluntly. "Doesn't take a scholar to see how this ends badly for everyone involved."

Ava turned to him, exasperation flickering in her gaze. "You're missing the point. This wasn't just violence for the sake of it. It was a test—a way to prove the bearer's worth."

Damian shrugged, his tone pragmatic. "Maybe. Or maybe it's just a reminder that power always comes with a price. Either way, I'm betting whoever carved this didn't survive to tell the tale."

Their differing approaches—Ava's intellectual curiosity and Damian's hardened realism—clashed, but it was the balance between them that made their partnership work. She saw meaning where he saw danger, and together, they uncovered truths neither could face alone.

Damian's fingers traced the ancient text, his brow furrowed in concentration. "It speaks of the Key of Anahita," he said, his voice low and grave. "The amulet's power can only be controlled with it. Without the key, chaos follows."

CHAPTER THREE: THE SECRETS BENEATH

Ava inhaled sharply. "That's what my father was after," she whispered. The puzzle pieces began to align—her father's obsession wasn't just about finding the amulet but ensuring it didn't fall into the wrong hands. Her father's last journal entries mentioned a man named Elliot Maddox, a name Damian had recognized with visible disdain when she first shared the fragments.

Before they could delve further, the sound of shouts echoed through the corridors. Damian tensed, his hand moving instinctively to the hilt of his blade. "We're not alone," he growled.

The shouts grew louder, boots pounding against the stone as the mercenaries closed in. Damian's blade was out in an instant, his body coiled like a predator ready to strike. Ava grabbed a jagged piece of rock from the floor, her pulse hammering in her ears.

Seconds later, a group of mercenaries stormed into the chamber, their weapons drawn. Ava and Damian were forced into a chaotic fight, dodging bullets and using the temple's narrow pathways to their advantage. Ava's agility and Damian's brute strength proved a formidable combination, but they were outnumbered. In the fray, Damian shielded Ava from a knife aimed at her back, taking a deep gash to his arm. "We're not going to win this!" Ava shouted, dodging a bullet that ricocheted off the stone wall beside her.

"Stay close!" Damian barked, his voice cutting through the chaos. He blocked a knife aimed at Ava, the blade slicing his arm instead. Blood seeped through his shirt, but he didn't falter, his focus unwavering. The fight was relentless, each movement a desperate bid for survival. Despite the odds, their coordination was seamless—Damian's brute force counterbalancing Ava's quick thinking. When the mercenaries finally retreated, it was clear they hadn't won the fight but merely survived it.

After a grueling struggle, the mercenaries retreated, leaving Ava and Damian battered but alive. As they leaned against the chamber wall, catching their breath, Ava noticed the gash on Damian's arm. Crimson streaks trickled down his bicep, his skin glistening with sweat and dirt. Without thinking, she tore a strip from her shirt, the fabric fraying under her hands.

"Hold still," she murmured, her voice firm yet betraying the concern she couldn't mask.

Damian winced but complied, his broad shoulders relaxing slightly against the wall. His gray eyes never left her face as she worked, her fingers trembling slightly as she wrapped the makeshift bandage around his arm. The proximity between them felt charged, every brush of her fingers against his skin sending a ripple of awareness through both of them.

"You're good at this," he said softly, his voice laced with gratitude and something deeper.

Ava tied the strip tightly, her lips quirking into a faint smile. "Comes with the territory," she replied. "Archaeology isn't all ancient scrolls and dusty tombs. Sometimes it's knives and bad luck."

Damian chuckled, though the sound was rough, laced with exhaustion. "Guess that explains why you're still standing."

Ava glanced up, meeting his gaze. His eyes held an intensity that made her breath catch, a quiet storm of emotions she couldn't quite name. Gratitude, yes, but also desire, raw and unguarded. His hand moved, tentative at first, brushing a loose strand of hair from her cheek. His touch was calloused but gentle, and the simple gesture sent a shiver down her spine.

"I couldn't let them hurt you," Damian said, his voice low and

CHAPTER THREE: THE SECRETS BENEATH

rough, the sincerity in his words cutting through her defenses.

Her chest tightened, a knot of emotions she'd buried for too long rising to the surface. The fear, the adrenaline, the unspoken connection that had been building between them—it all came crashing down. Without thinking, Ava leaned in, her lips finding his in a kiss that was both desperate and deliberate. The taste of him—salt, sweat, and something uniquely Damian—flooded her senses, and for a moment, the world outside the chamber ceased to exist.

Damian responded immediately, his hand moving to cradle the back of her neck, pulling her closer. The kiss deepened, growing more fervent, their breath mingling as their bodies pressed together. Ava straddled him, her thighs tightening around his hips as his hands slid down to grip her waist. The feel of his touch ignited something primal within her, a fire that burned away the doubts and fears that had been haunting her.

Her hands moved of their own accord, tugging at the tattered remains of his shirt. She exposed the hard lines of his chest, her fingertips tracing the ridges of old scars and the taut muscles beneath. Damian groaned at her touch, his control slipping as Ava took the lead. Her lips left a trail of kisses along his jaw, down his neck, and across his collarbone, savoring the heat of his skin beneath her mouth.

"Ava," Damian murmured, his voice breaking on her name. His hands roamed her body, skimming her back and sliding to her hips, their grip firm yet reverent.

Her breath hitched as she leaned into him, the tension building between them overwhelming. She kissed her way back up, reclaiming his lips with a fervor that spoke of months of loneliness, fear, and longing. Damian responded in kind, his hands anchoring her against him as their bodies moved in perfect sync.

The ancient chamber seemed to hold its breath, the flickering torchlight casting shadows over their entwined forms. The weight of their mission, the chaos of the outside world, faded to nothing as they gave themselves over to the moment. Damian surrendered to her completely, letting Ava take control, her dominance both thrilling and grounding.

Her fingers tangled in his hair as her body pressed against his, her movements deliberate and commanding. Damian groaned, his head falling back against the wall as she took what she wanted, his own desire evident in the way he responded to her every touch. Together, they found a rhythm, a timeless dance that echoed through the chamber.

As the intensity built, their whispered names and soft gasps mingled with the crackle of the torches. Ava felt a sense of power unlike anything she'd ever known, the knowledge that Damian—this strong, unyielding man—had placed himself completely in her hands.

When the final crescendo hit, it was as if the world shattered and rebuilt itself in that singular moment. Their breathing slowed, their bodies still entwined as they rested against the stone wall, the heat of their connection lingering in the air.

Damian brushed his lips against her temple, his voice soft and filled with wonder. "You're full of surprises, Red."

Ava chuckled, her head resting against his shoulder. "You haven't seen anything yet."

For a moment, they stayed like that, holding each other in the flickering light. But the danger outside the chamber was never far from their minds, and they both knew this fragile peace wouldn't last.

"We should move," Ava said finally, her voice steady but reluctant.

Damian nodded, his hand lingering on her waist as they stood. Their bond, now solidified in ways neither could have predicted, was both a strength and a vulnerability they couldn't afford to ignore.

The Betrayal and Rescue

The intimacy of their moment was shattered when a voice rang out. "Well, well, Damian Cross," a man sneered. "Still playing the hero?"

Damian froze, his eyes narrowing. "Elliot." The name was laced with contempt.

Elliot Maddox, a former comrade from Damian's mercenary days, stepped out of the shadows, flanked by armed men. His cocky smirk and sharp eyes betrayed his intentions. "You always were sentimental," Elliot said, his gaze flickering to Ava. "And now you're chasing trinkets for your latest cause."

Damian's body tensed. "What do you want, Elliot?"

Elliot's smirk turned cold. "The amulet, of course. And the map she's carrying. Let's not forget I was the one who first heard about the Key of Anahita. Your little archaeologist's daddy had loose lips, and I made sure he shared enough before he conveniently disappeared."

Ava's blood ran cold. "You knew my father?" she hissed.

Elliot chuckled. "Knew him? Sweetheart, I worked with him. Or rather, I used him. He was too idealistic for this game. Couldn't make the hard choices." His gaze hardened as it shifted back to Damian. "And speaking of hard choices, it's nice to see you've found another way to disappoint."

The betrayal stung, but there was no time to dwell. Ava and Damian were subdued and dragged to an interrogation room within the temple. Elliot wasted no time, his questions sharp and his threats sharper. He relished in taunting Damian, poking at old wounds. "Still chasing redemption, Cross? Some of us moved on from our guilt and made something of ourselves."

When Elliot left to retrieve reinforcements, Ava leaned into Damian. "I have an idea," she whispered. Using her agility and the sharp edge of a relic fragment, she cut through her bindings. Damian followed her lead, his strength a crucial asset as they overpowered their captors and slipped out of the room. Ava's heart pounded as she slipped her bindings, the sharp edge of the relic cutting through the rope. She glanced at Damian, who gave her a subtle nod before springing into action.

The chaos that followed was a blur of movement and sound—Ava's quick thinking and Damian's brute strength making them an unstoppable force. She ducked under a swinging baton, delivering a swift blow to her attacker's knee, while Damian disarmed another with a single punch.

When they finally burst into the open air, Ava felt an unfamiliar rush of confidence. She wasn't just surviving—she was fighting back.

As they fled the temple, she glanced at Damian, his determination mirroring her own. For the first time, she realized this wasn't just about her father's legacy—it was about reclaiming her own strength.

Their escape was perilous, fraught with near misses and narrow escapes. Ava's ingenuity and Damian's strength made them an unstoppable team, their trust in each other solidifying despite the odds. As they fled the temple, Ava's confidence surged. For the first time, she felt like she wasn't just chasing her father's ghost—she was confronting the forces that had torn her life apart.

4

Chapter Four: Desires and Deception

Seduction Under the Stars

Ava and Damian trudged deeper into the jungle, the moonlight filtering through the canopy to cast a soft glow on the foliage around them. The adrenaline of their escape had given way to exhaustion, and when they stumbled upon a hidden grove, its calmness was too inviting to pass.

The grove was enchanting—surrounded by thick ferns and illuminated by the silver light of the moon. A small stream trickled nearby, its gentle sound soothing their frayed nerves. Damian dropped his gear and leaned against a moss-covered rock, his shirt stained with dried blood from his earlier wound. Ava knelt beside him, inspecting the bandage she had hastily tied.

"This will hold," she said, her voice barely above a whisper. "But you need proper stitching."

"I've had worse," Damian muttered, his tone soft but edged

with fatigue. He studied her face, noticing the tension in her brow. "What about you? How are you holding up?"

Ava hesitated, then sat beside him. Her gaze lingered on the stream, as if it held the answers to her racing thoughts. "Sometimes I wonder if I'm any different from my father," she admitted. "He was consumed by this quest, and it destroyed him. What if I'm heading down the same path?"

Damian reached out, his hand brushing hers. "You're not your father, Ava. You're stronger, sharper. You see the dangers he overlooked."

His words brought her comfort, and she turned to him, her eyes searching his face. "What about you, Damian? What keeps you going?"

Damian glanced at the stream, his expression softening as he reflected. "You know, before all this, I believed I was defined by the shadows I came from—the bad choices, the lives I couldn't save. But now..." He trailed off, his gaze locking with hers. "I'm starting to think I might be more than that."

The raw vulnerability in his voice stirred something in Ava. "You are," she said firmly, her voice unwavering. "You're stronger than your past."

He let out a heavy sigh, his expression darkening. "Regret, mostly. I've done things I'm not proud of. Lost people I cared about. Sometimes I think helping you find this amulet is my way of making up for it."

The vulnerability in his voice stirred something deep within her. Ava leaned closer, her hand resting on his chest, feeling the steady beat of his heart. "We've both lost pieces of ourselves," she murmured. "Maybe we can help each other find what's left."

The intimacy of the moment deepened as their lips met in a

CHAPTER FOUR: DESIRES AND DECEPTION

slow, deliberate kiss. Ava climbed into his lap, her hands trailing down his chest as his fingers tangled in her hair. This time, there was no hesitation, only the surrender to a need that had been building between them.

She guided him onto the mossy ground, her dominance asserting itself in the way she moved, her lips and hands exploring every inch of him. Damian responded with a mix of restraint and fervor, allowing Ava to take control while reveling in the intimacy they shared. Their passion was both tender and intense, a balance of vulnerability and power that left them breathless beneath the stars.

An Unexpected Ally

The sun was just beginning to rise when they heard the crunch of footsteps in the underbrush. Ava and Damian tensed, their weapons drawn, but the figure that emerged wasn't a threat—or at least not immediately.

"Easy there," the woman said, holding her hands up in mock surrender. She was tall and striking, with auburn hair that caught the early light and sharp green eyes that missed nothing. "You look like you've been through hell."

"And who are you?" Damian demanded, his tone wary.

"Elena Vega," she replied smoothly. "Historian. And, as luck would have it, someone who knows a thing or two about the Amulet of Ixchel."

Elena leaned casually against a nearby tree, her posture exuding confidence. "You're wondering why I'm here. It's not just about the amulet. It never is."

Ava folded her arms. "Then enlighten us."

Elena chuckled, a low, sultry sound. "Let's just say, I know what it's like to be desperate for answers. I grew up watching my father sacrifice everything for his archaeological pursuits. He died penniless, obsessed with treasures that never brought him peace. So now, I make sure every risk I take is worth it."

The mention of her father softened Ava's suspicion, if only slightly. Elena tilted her head toward Damian, her smirk returning. "And Damian, well, he and I go way back. He taught me how to survive this world. Didn't you, Cross?"

Damian's jaw tightened, his tone curt. "We worked together, that's all."

As Damian pulled his arm away, Elena stepped closer, her voice dropping. "Don't pretend we didn't have something, Damian. You may try to run from it, but we both know it's still there."

Damian's gaze hardened. "Whatever we had ended the moment you chose yourself over everyone else."

Elena's smile faltered, the vulnerability flashing in her eyes so brief it was almost imperceptible. She recovered quickly, her smirk sharper. "Suit yourself. But remember, trust is a luxury none of us can afford."

Ava watched the exchange with a growing sense of unease, her distrust of Elena deepening. As Elena deciphered the carvings, she paused, her fingers lingering over an intricate glyph. "These traps aren't just meant to deter. They're tests of loyalty, patience, and sacrifice."

"What are you saying?" Ava asked, narrowing her eyes.

Elena straightened, a glint of determination in her eyes. "Whoever hid the Key of Anahita didn't just want to protect it. They wanted to ensure only someone worthy could claim it. And worth, as I've learned, is subjective."

CHAPTER FOUR: DESIRES AND DECEPTION

Damian scoffed. "You sound like one of the zealots who carved this place."

Elena's gaze flickered to him, her smile bittersweet. "Maybe they weren't wrong.

The command room was suffocating, a low-ceilinged bunker hidden deep within the jungle's dense foliage. The air was damp, heavy with the scent of mildew and old leather. A single overhead lamp flickered, casting erratic shadows over the rough-hewn wooden table where a map of the jungle sprawled. Dozens of markings crisscrossed the map—coordinates, hastily scrawled notes, and trails that led to dead ends. Empty coffee cups and a half-eaten meal sat discarded on the edges, signs of Elliot's obsessive focus on the hunt for the Amulet of Ixchel.

Elliot Maddox leaned back in his chair, his sharp suit now rumpled, though it did little to diminish the aura of authority he carried. His fingers drummed against the map as he studied the newest report from his mercenaries. The tension in the room was palpable, a quiet hum of anticipation hanging over the small group gathered around him.

"They're getting closer," one of his mercenaries reported. The mercenary, clad in worn tactical gear, shifted on his feet as if nervous to deliver bad news. Elliot smirked. "Good. Let them do the hard work. Once they find the amulet, we'll strike."

A woman stepped forward—Elena. "You're underestimating Ava," she said. Elliot's smirk widened. "No, Elena. I'm counting on her. She'll lead me straight to the prize."

This proves Elliot's manipulative nature and sets up tension for the final confrontation. Elliot and Elena's dynamic share a history of manipulation and mutual reliance, with Elena working alongside Elliot out of pragmatism rather than loyalty. This adds depth to her betrayal later and sets up her eventual split from Elliot.

Ava exchanged a glance with Damian, her instincts screaming caution. "How do you know about the amulet?"

Elena smirked. "Let's just say I've been chasing its trail longer than you have. I've seen the temple you just left, by the way—nasty work, those mercenaries. Lucky for you, I'm not one of them."

Despite her charm, Ava felt an immediate dislike for Elena. The way her gaze lingered on Damian didn't help. Over the course of their conversation, Elena flirted shamelessly, her tone playful as she leaned closer to him than necessary.

"I must say," Elena purred, her fingers brushing Damian's arm as she examined his bandaged wound, "you're quite the survivor. Most men wouldn't have made it out of that temple."

Damian stiffened, clearly uncomfortable with her attention, but Ava's irritation flared. "We don't have time for games," Ava snapped, stepping between them. "If you know something about the amulet, start talking."

Elena raised an eyebrow, her smirk deepening. "Feisty. I like that. Fine. The amulet's power is useless without the Key of Anahita. And I know where to find it." Damian's wariness of Elena, his subtle accusations and avoidance of her advances show he doesn't fully trust her, reinforcing the triangle of tension between Damian, Elena, and Ava.

CHAPTER FOUR: DESIRES AND DECEPTION

The Path to the Key

Following Elena's guidance, they trekked to a remote underwater cavern. Elena explained that the key had been hidden there centuries ago, protected by traps designed to deter all but the most determined seekers. As Elena deciphered the carvings, she paused, her fingers lingering over an intricate glyph. "These traps aren't just meant to deter. They're tests of loyalty, patience, and sacrifice."

"What are you saying?" Ava asked, narrowing her eyes.

Elena straightened, a glint of determination in her eyes. "Whoever hid the Key of Anahita didn't just want to protect it. They wanted to ensure only someone worthy could claim it. And worth, as I've learned, is subjective."

Damian scoffed. "You sound like one of the zealots who carved this place."

Elena's gaze flickered to him, her smile bittersweet. "Maybe they weren't wrong."

The cavern was breathtaking, its entrance concealed by a waterfall that glittered in the sunlight. Inside, the water glowed with an otherworldly blue light, illuminating ancient carvings on the walls. But the beauty was deceptive—the trio quickly encountered a series of deadly traps, from collapsing walls to hidden spikes.

Elena's expertise proved invaluable as she deciphered the carvings, guiding them through the labyrinthine passages. However, her boldness bordered on recklessness. At one point, she triggered a trap that nearly crushed Ava, and only Damian's quick reflexes saved her.

"Watch yourself!" Damian snapped, his protective instincts flaring. "You almost got her killed."

Elena shrugged, unrepentant. "Calculated risk. You're welcome, by the way, for getting us this far."

A Twist of Betrayal

When they finally reached the chamber holding the key, the tension between the trio was palpable. The Key of Anahita rested on a pedestal, its intricate design gleaming in the soft light. But as Ava reached for it, Elena's demeanor shifted.

"Sorry, sweetheart," Elena said, her voice laced with mock regret. "But this is where we part ways."

In a swift motion, Elena drew a hidden weapon and activated a trap, sealing Ava and Damian inside the chamber as she fled with the key. "Give my regards to the mercenaries," she called over her shoulder.

As Elena held the weapon steady, her voice wavered for the first time. "You think I wanted this? That I enjoy betraying the only people who ever gave a damn about me?" She gestured toward the sealed chamber, her smirk fading. "This world doesn't reward loyalty, Ava. It devours it. I chose to survive."

Ava's voice was sharp, her anger barely contained. "And what's survival worth when you've sold your soul?"

Elena's lips pressed into a thin line, her eyes glistening with unspoken emotion. "More than you'd think."

The betrayal was a brutal blow, but as Ava and Damian worked together to escape the trap, their bond only deepened. They knew now that the stakes were higher than ever, and their trust in each other was the only thing that could see them through.

5

Chapter Five: Shadows of the Past

The Aftermath of Betrayal

Ava and Damian sat in the dim cavern chamber, their breaths harsh and labored after narrowly escaping Elena's trap. Dust and debris from the triggered mechanism still hung in the air, swirling in the faint beams of light filtering through cracks in the walls. As Ava and Damian traversed a narrow jungle path, the ground beneath Ava's feet gave way. She grabbed a vine, dangling precariously over a pit of jagged rocks. Damian's voice was steady but urgent. "Hold on, I've got you!"

He pulled her to safety just as the vine began to fray. "The jungle isn't just trying to kill us," Ava panted, her heart pounding. "It's testing us."

This scene intensifies the setting and aligns with the shaman's warning about proving one's worth.

"Damn her," Ava hissed, her fists clenching as she paced. The memory of Elena's smirk as she escaped with the Key of Anahita burned in her mind. "I should have known she was playing us."

Damian wiped blood from a shallow cut on his temple, his voice calm but edged with steel. "Elena doesn't act without reason. Someone paid her well, and I'd bet my life it's the same collector Elliot's working for."

At the mention of Elliot, a dark shadow passed over Damian's face. Ava noticed and stepped closer. "You need to tell me everything about him," she said firmly. "If he's tied to my father, I need to know what we're up against."

Damian nodded, his shoulders heavy with the weight of the past as Elliot Maddox wasn't just a mercenary commander—he was a strategist, a manipulator who thrived on chaos. His network spanned continents, with ties to black-market collectors, rogue governments, and criminal syndicates. Though his team of mercenaries executed his plans, they weren't his only weapon. Elliot operated like a spider in a web, pulling strings from the shadows and anticipating every move his adversaries might make. Damian started "Elliot and I...we were brothers in everything but blood. We worked together for years—until greed got the better of him. He betrayed our team, sold us out to the highest bidder. Half the squad died because of his choice." His jaw tightened. "Your father...he was part of that fallout. Elliot used him, wringing every ounce of knowledge from him about the amulet before leaving him to die." The mercenaries under his command were well-trained and ruthless, but whispers in the underworld hinted at something more sinister: that Elliot wasn't the real power. He was the enforcer of a shadowy collector whose obsession with the Amulet of Ixchel rivaled Ava's father's. This collector funded Elliot's operations, ensuring no expense was spared in the pursuit of the amulet.

"He's not just a threat because of his men," Damian said as

they moved through the jungle. "Elliot knows how to get inside your head. He'll use whatever you care about most against you."

The revelation sent a chill down Ava's spine. Her father's mysterious disappearance now made a grim kind of sense. "So, this isn't just about the amulet for Elliot. It's personal."

Damian met her gaze. "It's always personal with Elliot."

A Reluctant Alliance

Determined to retrieve the key and stop Elena from delivering it to Elliot's shadowy employer, Ava and Damian pushed deeper into the jungle. They moved with urgency, their bond strengthened by shared purpose and the lingering heat of their previous intimacy.

The jungle was unforgiving—thick with tangled vines and the distant growl of predators. They tracked Elena's trail with a mix of Damian's survival skills and Ava's sharp instincts, eventually arriving at a hidden airstrip carved into the jungle floor. The airstrip was a crude but functional clearing carved out of the jungle, the uneven ground reinforced with steel plates and surrounded by hastily erected watchtowers. Cargo crates, fuel drums, and ammunition boxes were stacked in organized chaos, the scene lit by the harsh glow of floodlights.

Mercenaries moved like clockwork, their movements efficient as they prepared to load supplies onto a single-engine aircraft parked at the edge of the strip. The low hum of the plane's idling engine added to the tension, a constant reminder that time was running out.

From their vantage point in the foliage, Ava could see the pilots securing flight charts while guards patrolled the perimeter with military precision. The jungle beyond was a sea of shadows, but the floodlights made every inch of the airstrip glaringly visible—a dangerous terrain for anyone hoping to infiltrate undetected.

"We'll only get one shot at this," Damian whispered, his gaze sharp as he assessed the scene.

Ava nodded, her heart pounding. "Then we make it count." There, they found the mercenaries, preparing to load supplies onto a small aircraft.

"They're regrouping," Damian muttered, his hand tightening on his weapon. "Elliot's sending them back to secure the amulet."

Ava's gaze darted to the plane. "We can't let them leave."

Together, they ambushed the mercenaries in a tense, high-stakes fight. The airstrip erupted in chaos—bullets flew, crates shattered, and the jungle itself seemed to conspire against them. Ava's determination shone as she outmaneuvered her opponents, while Damian's combat skills were a lethal symphony of precision and power.

When the dust settled, they interrogated the last conscious mercenary. He revealed that Elena was heading to a remote stronghold—a compound where Elliot planned to meet her and claim the key. The key glinted in the moonlight, its intricate carvings catching the silvery glow as Ava held it in trembling hands. She traced the design with her fingers, her breath hitching as the weight of its significance settled over her.

"We did it," she whispered, her voice breaking with emotion. For a moment, the exhaustion and pain of the day faded, replaced by a surge of triumph that brought tears to her eyes.

Damian stood beside her, his own weariness momentarily forgotten as he watched her. "You did it," he said softly, a rare smile tugging at his lips. "Your father would be proud."

CHAPTER FIVE: SHADOWS OF THE PAST

Ava turned to him, her heart full. "We did this together," she said firmly.

Without thinking, she threw her arms around him, her relief spilling over into the embrace. Damian hesitated for a fraction of a second before wrapping his arms around her, the warmth of the moment cutting through the cold realities of their situation.

As they pulled apart, their eyes met, a silent understanding passing between them. For the first time, the elusive sense of closure felt within reach, even as the dangers ahead loomed large.

In the aftermath, Ava and Damian escape with the key, their partnership strengthened but their wounds—both physical and emotional—still raw. The jungle feels like a sanctuary compared to the stronghold's suffocating tension. As they plan their next move, Ava looks at Damian and sees not just a mercenary but a man fighting his own battles, much like her. "We can't do this alone," she says softly. Damian nods, his gaze steady. "Then we won't."

The Stronghold and the Seduction

Under the light of a full moon, Ava and Damian shared a quiet moment by the river. "Why do you keep calling me Red?" Ava asked, her tone teasing. Damian's smirk softened. "Because fire suits you—fierce, unyielding, and impossible to ignore."

Ava blushed but didn't look away. "And you? Always the lone wolf?" Damian's expression grew serious. "Not anymore," he said, his voice barely above a whisper. The tension between them broke as their lips met, the kiss both a promise and a release.

This scene deepens their bond and provides a respite from the relentless action.

Ava and Damian approached the stronghold, a crumbling fortress perched atop a cliff. The air was electric with anticipation and the lingering tension between them. Damian's gaze lingered on Ava as she checked her gear, her fiery determination captivating him.

"You're incredible, Red," he murmured, his nickname for her laced with admiration. Ava paused, her lips curving into a faint smile.

"So are you," she replied, her voice softer. "We make a hell of a team."

The moment stretched, charged with unspoken emotions and the undercurrent of their desire. Damian reached for her, pulling her close. Their kiss was slow but fierce, a collision of passion and fear—a reminder that every moment might be their last. Ava's dominance surfaced as she pushed Damian against the rough stone wall, her lips and hands exploring him with an intensity that left him breathless.

"Focus, Cross," she whispered against his ear, her voice a blend of command and teasing. "We've got a job to do."

They broke apart, their resolve steeled by the connection they shared.

Confronting Elena and Elliot

The stronghold's interior was an eerie mix of decay and grandeur. Moonlight filtered through broken windows, illuminating the dust swirling in the air. They moved silently, their steps muffled on the stone floor. The tension was palpable as they approached a set of heavy wooden doors. Damian pushed them open carefully, revealing a lavishly decorated study.

CHAPTER FIVE: SHADOWS OF THE PAST

Elena Vega sat comfortably in a high-backed chair, a glass of wine in hand. Her lips curved into a satisfied smirk as she spotted them. On the table beside her, the Key of Anahita glinted in the dim light.

"Ah, my favorite duo," Elena greeted, her tone dripping with mockery. "I must say, you've been rather persistent."

Ava's fury erupted, her voice sharp. "You lied to us. Played us. You nearly got us killed."

Elena raised an eyebrow, her smirk deepening. "Oh, darling, don't take it personally. Business is business. And the collector pays very well."

Damian stepped forward, his voice low and menacing. "You've chosen the wrong side, Elena."

Before Elena could respond, another voice cut through the tension. "On the contrary, she's exactly where she needs to be."

Elena's escape was as calculated as it was desperate. As Damian and Ava's attention was drawn to Elliot's arrival, she moved with the precision of someone who had navigated such betrayals before. Her hands worked quickly, releasing a small, concealed smoke bomb that filled the room with a blinding white cloud.

Ava coughed, her eyes stinging as she swung blindly at the sound of footsteps. "Elena!" she shouted, her voice cutting through the haze.

But by the time the smoke cleared, Elena was gone. The sound of her boots against the metal floor faded into the jungle, swallowed by the cacophony of insects and distant growls.

Elena's heart pounded as she sprinted through the underbrush, clutching the stolen artifact to her chest. She didn't stop until she reached a moss-covered pillar deep in the jungle, her breath coming in ragged gasps.

For a moment, she leaned against the stone, her fingers brushing over the carvings on the key. The weight of her choices pressed heavily on her chest. "Survival first," she muttered, though the words sounded hollow even to her ears.

She glanced back toward the airstrip, guilt flickering in her emerald eyes. But the pull of the amulet's secrets—and the promise of its power—was too strong. With a final, resolute breath, she disappeared into the night, her path diverging from Ava and Damian's once again.

Elliot Maddox strode into the room, his presence commanding and his expression coldly amused. His tailored clothing and composed demeanor stood in stark contrast to the crumbling surroundings. He gave Damian a once-over, his smirk sharp. "Still trying to play the hero, Cross?"

The air grew heavier as the confrontation escalated. Damian's fists clenched, his jaw tightening as Elliot's taunts dredged up old wounds. "You always were a coward, Elliot," Damian growled. "Hiding behind others to do your dirty work."

Elliot's smirk faded, replaced by a glare. "And you always were a fool. Sacrificing yourself for people who'd throw you away without a second thought."

Meanwhile, Ava's attention shifted to Elena. The betrayal cut deep, but it was the glint in Elena's eyes—some mix of guilt and defiance—that stoked Ava's anger. "You could have chosen to help us," Ava snapped. "But you sided with him."

Elena rose gracefully, setting her wine glass down. "I chose survival, Ava. You should try it sometime. It's surprisingly liberating."

The tension broke like a thunderclap. Damian lunged at Elliot, their clash raw and unrelenting. Fists and fury collided as years of betrayal and regret poured into each strike. Elliot fought with calculated precision, but Damian's rage made him a relentless force.

On the other side of the room, Ava and Elena squared off. Their struggle wasn't just physical; it was a battle of ideals and emotions. Elena's movements were fluid, her strikes controlled, but Ava's determination and anger gave her an edge.

"You think you're better than me?" Elena hissed, her voice sharp with envy. "You're just like the rest of us—chasing something you'll never hold on to."

"I'd rather fight for something real than sell out for survival," Ava shot back, her voice shaking with emotion. "At least I'm not afraid of my own choices."

As the fights raged, the room became a maelstrom of chaos and emotion. Damian's final blow sent Elliot sprawling to the ground, blood trickling from the corner of his mouth. He glared up at Damian, his voice cold and deliberate. "This isn't over."

Elena, seeing the tide turn, disengaged from Ava and darted toward the Key of Anahita. Damian intercepted her, grabbing her wrist just before she could snatch it. "You're done here, Elena," he said, his voice firm.

For a moment, something flickered in Elena's eyes—remorse, perhaps, or resignation. But it was gone as quickly as it appeared. "We'll see," she said softly before pulling free and vanishing into the shadows.

A Fight for Legacy

After escaping the mercenaries, Elena leaned against a moss-covered pillar, her hands trembling. The memory of Ava's fiery determination flashed in her mind, followed by Elliot's cold, calculating gaze. She clenched her fist. Survival always came first, but this time, it didn't feel right. This really humanizes Elena, hinting at an internal conflict that could lead to future redemption or betrayal. When Elliot ordered his guards to seize Ava and Damian, the room erupted into chaos. The fight was brutal and raw, with Damian facing his former comrade in a battle years in the making. Their blows carried the weight of betrayal and regret, each man fighting not just to win but to prove something to himself.

Ava faced Elena, their clash as much about their warring ideals as it was about survival. Elena's cunning was matched by Ava's determination, and as the fight wore on, it became clear that Ava's resolve to honor her father's legacy was unshakable.

In the end, Ava and Damian emerged victorious. Elliot lay unconscious, and Elena, realizing she'd lost, made another desperate escape. The Key of Anahita was still theirs.

Obsession and Redemption

As dawn broke over the jungle, Ava and Damian stood together, the key glinting in her hands. Their journey was far from over, but for the first time, Ava felt a sense of closure—not just for her father's disappearance but for her own search for purpose.

Damian, his wounds both physical and emotional, found solace in Ava's presence. Their connection was no longer just about survival or passion—it was about trust, something neither of them had known in years.

"Where do we go from here?" Ava asked softly.

"Wherever you lead, Red," Damian replied, his voice filled with quiet certainty.

CHAPTER FIVE: SHADOWS OF THE PAST

The amulet's secrets beckoned, and their shared legacy awaited, but for now, they had each other—and that was enough.

6

Chapter Six: Whispers in the Shadows

The dense jungle closed in around them as the sun dipped lower on the horizon, casting long shadows that danced ominously. Ava focused on the stone tablet in front of her, running her fingers along the worn etchings as Damian stood watch nearby. The coded messages etched into the ancient stones spoke of trials and hidden paths, their cryptic nature fueling her determination. Ava crouched beside the stone tablet, her fingers tracing the carved symbols as Damian stood watch nearby. The jungle pressed close around them, alive with the sounds of chirping insects and distant animal calls. The faint orange glow of the setting sun filtered through the dense canopy, casting an otherworldly light over the ruins.

"Got it," Ava muttered, her voice taut with focus. She pointed to a glyph near the bottom of the tablet. "This symbol. It's a directional marker."

Damian peered over her shoulder, his tall frame casting a shadow over her. "You sure?"

"Positive," Ava replied, standing and brushing dirt from her pants. "It's pointing to Chachapoyas."

CHAPTER SIX: WHISPERS IN THE SHADOWS

"Chachapoyas?" Damian repeated, raising an eyebrow. "The Cloud Warriors?"

"Yes." Ava nodded, excitement creeping into her voice. "It's an ancient city nestled in the mountains. My father's notes mentioned it briefly—a place tied to the final resting place of the Amulet of Ixchel."

Damian nodded, his gaze scanning the jungle. "Then we move."

The Hidden City of Chachapoyas

The journey to Chachapoyas was grueling, the dense jungle giving way to steep mountain paths that tested their endurance. By the time they reached the city's outskirts, dawn had broken, bathing the ruins in a pale golden light. The air here was crisp, cooler than the oppressive humidity of the jungle. Mist clung to the ground, curling around the ancient stone structures that rose from the mountainside like forgotten sentinels.

Chachapoyas was breathtaking. The city's crumbling walls were etched with carvings depicting warriors and gods, their stern faces staring out at the valley below. Vines snaked through the ruins, reclaiming the stone, while wildflowers bloomed in vivid bursts of color, softening the starkness of the ancient architecture.

"Your father was here," Damian said, his voice breaking the reverent silence.

Ava knelt to examine a faded inscription on a pillar, her heart pounding. "He was. This is where he believed the key's power could be activated."

As they moved deeper into the ruins, the sound of footsteps echoed through the still air. Ava and Damian spun, their weapons drawn, as a figure emerged from the shadows of a crumbling archway.

A New Ally?

The woman was striking, her auburn hair catching the morning light. She was dressed practically, in sturdy boots and a fitted jacket, but there was an air of refinement about her that set her apart from the rugged landscape. Her piercing green eyes locked onto Ava with a mix of curiosity and recognition.

"You must be Ava Whitmore," she said, her tone confident. "Your father spoke of you often."

Ava's breath caught. "Who are you?"

The woman stepped closer, her movements smooth and deliberate. "Dr. Marisol Carranza. Archaeologist, historian, and someone who's been tracking Elliot Maddox as long as you have."

Damian frowned, his weapon still raised. "And why should we trust you?"

Marisol held her hands up, palms open in a gesture of peace. "Because I knew your father, Ava. We worked together before he disappeared. He entrusted me with part of his research, including a lead on the Key of Anahita."

"Why haven't I heard of you before?" Ava asked, her voice edged with suspicion.

Marisol's gaze softened. "Your father didn't want you involved in his work. He wanted to keep you safe. But after what happened to him, I couldn't stay on the sidelines."

CHAPTER SIX: WHISPERS IN THE SHADOWS

Marisol's Connection

As the trio worked to decipher the next clue, Marisol's expertise became apparent. She moved through the room with practiced ease, her knowledge of the symbols and their meanings outpacing even Ava's. Together, they pieced together a series of instructions leading to the amulet's final location: an underwater temple hidden within the Utcubamba River valley.

Damian leaned against the wall, his gray eyes fixed on Marisol. "You seem awfully prepared for someone who just 'happened' to find us."

Marisol smirked, her confidence unshaken. "Let's just say I've been following the breadcrumbs longer than you've been holding a machete." Their progress was interrupted by the sound of distant engines. The rumble grew louder, reverberating off the stone walls, until a group of mercenaries burst into the ruins. Their rifles gleamed in the sunlight, their black uniforms marking them as Elliot's men.

"Get down!" Damian barked, pulling Ava behind a stone column as bullets ricocheted around them.

Marisol grabbed a relic from the pedestal, using it to smash through a concealed door. "This way!" she shouted.

The trio fled through the hidden passage, the mercenaries close on their heels. The narrow tunnel twisted and turned, the light from their torches barely illuminating the path ahead. Finally, they emerged into a hidden cavern, its walls glowing with the faint luminescence of bioluminescent moss.

The mercenaries' pursuit had ceased, their shouts fading into the distance. Ava collapsed against the wall, her chest heaving as she caught her breath. Damian leaned beside her, his expression tense but focused.

Flirting with Shadows

Later that evening, Ava drew Damian aside, ostensibly to discuss strategy. Their conversation quickly turned personal as she brought up their past, her tone shifting between nostalgic and provocative.

"You know, we made a good team," Ava said, leaning against a moss-covered column. "If things had been different..." Damian cut her off, his tone firm. "You chose your side Ava."

"Right on your side, here I am," she countered, stepping closer. "Maybe I made the wrong choices earlier in life."

Ava, unable to help herself, followed the sound of their voices. She caught enough of their conversation to fuel her doubts, and when Damian returned to the campfire, she confronted him.

"Do you have history with everyone we meet?" Ava asked, her arms crossed tightly.

Damian sighed, running a hand through his hair. "Elena and I worked together a few times. That's it."

"Doesn't seem like that's how she sees it."

Damian stepped closer, his voice softening. "Ava, you know where I stand. Don't let her games mess with your head."

Their argument gave way to a charged silence, the tension breaking only when Damian reached for her. His lips captured hers in a kiss that was as much about reassurance as it was about desire. Their bodies pressed together, their connection solidifying as they sought comfort in each other.

The argument gave way to a charged silence, the tension between them crackling like a live wire in the cool night air. They stood under the remnants of a stone archway, its surface

CHAPTER SIX: WHISPERS IN THE SHADOWS

worn smooth by centuries of jungle rain and creeping moss. The flickering light from their campfire played over their faces, casting shadows that danced with the emotions neither could quite name. It was late, the air around them heavy with the sounds of the jungle: chirping crickets, distant howls, and the rustle of leaves stirred by the faintest of breezes.

Damian closed the small space between them, his tall frame a wall of heat and resolve. His steel-gray eyes met Ava's, softening just enough to let her see the vulnerability beneath his hard exterior. Without a word, he reached for her, his roughened hands cupping her face as he brought his lips to hers. The kiss was slow at first, a tentative exploration, but it quickly deepened, fueled by the frustration, desire, and unspoken fears they both carried.

Ava responded with equal fervor, her fingers threading through his dark hair as she pulled him closer. His hands slid down her neck to her shoulders, then to her waist, drawing her against him until there was no space left between their bodies. The kiss broke for a moment, their breaths mingling as Damian murmured, "I need you."

The words unlocked something in her, a deep and primal desire that had been simmering under the surface. Ava tugged at the hem of his shirt, pulling it over his head and exposing the hard planes of his chest. Her hands roamed over his warm skin, feeling the scars and strength that told the story of his life. Damian's lips found her neck, trailing heated kisses along her collarbone as his hands slipped beneath her shirt, exploring the soft curves of her body.

He lifted her with ease, her legs wrapping instinctively around his waist as he pressed her back against the ancient stone. The cool surface was a stark contrast to the heat building between them. Ava gasped as Damian's lips claimed hers again, his kiss now demanding and urgent. She arched into him, her fingers digging into his shoulders as his hands slid down to her thighs, holding her steady as his body pressed against hers.

Their movements grew more frantic, their need for each other overcoming any lingering hesitation. Damian's lips left a trail of fire down her neck and over the swell of her breast as he unfastened her bra with practiced ease. His mouth found her nipple, his tongue flicking over the sensitive peak and drawing a low moan from her lips.

Ava's hands found the buckle of his belt, her fingers working quickly to free him. Damian groaned as she reached beneath the fabric, her touch sending a jolt of pleasure through him. He pulled back just enough to lay her down on the soft grass at the base of the archway, the stars above casting a faint glow over their entwined bodies.

He took his time undressing her, his hands and lips worshiping every inch of her skin as he exposed it to the night air. Ava's breaths came in shallow gasps as his mouth trailed down her stomach, his touch both tender and insistent. When he reached the apex of her thighs, he paused, his eyes meeting hers with an intensity that made her heart race.

"You're beautiful," he murmured, his voice rough with need.

Before she could respond, his lips descended, and Ava's world narrowed to the sensation of Damian's mouth and the exquisite pleasure he drew from her body. She writhed beneath him, her fingers tangling in his hair as waves of sensation washed over her.

When he finally rose above her, his body aligning with hers, Ava pulled him down into another searing kiss. Their connection was electric, their movements synchronized as if they had done

CHAPTER SIX: WHISPERS IN THE SHADOWS

this a thousand times before. Damian entered her slowly, his groan mingling with Ava's sharp intake of breath. They moved together in a rhythm that was both primal and deeply intimate, their bodies speaking the words they couldn't say aloud.

The jungle around them seemed to fade, leaving only the two of them and the raw connection they shared. As they reached the peak of their passion, Ava clung to Damian, her nails digging into his back as her body trembled beneath his. He followed her over the edge moments later, his grip on her tightening as he buried his face in the crook of her neck.

They lay together in the aftermath, their bodies tangled and their breaths mingling in the humid air. Damian brushed a strand of hair from Ava's face, his expression uncharacteristically open. "Whatever happens," he said softly, "we'll face it together."

The night's intimacy lingered between them as they approached the secluded village hosting the masquerade. The vibrant masks and ceremonial attire of the villagers stood in stark contrast to the primal simplicity of the night before. Ava found herself stealing glances at Damian, the memory of their passion a constant hum beneath the surface of her thoughts.

Marisol, ever observant, noticed the shift in their dynamic immediately. "You two seem... close," she remarked, her tone teasing as they donned their own masks. Ava bristled but chose not to respond, her focus shifting to the task at hand.

The masquerade was unlike anything Ava had ever seen. The villagers moved with a practiced precision, their movements synchronized with the rhythm of the drums that echoed through the night. The air was thick with incense and mystery, the glow of torches casting flickering shadows over the gathering.

As the ceremonial dance began, Damian stepped into the circle, his movements hesitant at first but growing more confident as he followed the lead of the villagers. Marisol joined him, her steps bold and fluid, her body moving with a sensuality that drew attention.

Ava watched from the edge of the circle, her jaw tightening as Marisol's hand lingered on Damian's arm during a particularly close turn. The jealousy she had felt earlier returned with a vengeance, but she forced herself to focus on the figure standing apart from the crowd.

The cryptic figure's presence was magnetic, their simple mask and dark robes setting them apart from the elaborate attire of the villagers. When they motioned for Ava to follow, she hesitated only for a moment before slipping away from the circle. Whatever secrets they held, Ava was determined to uncover them—even if it meant confronting truths she wasn't ready to face.

Marisol stood at the entrance, her gaze scanning the jungle beyond. "They won't stop," she said, her voice steady. "Elliot's too close now. He'll do whatever it takes to find the amulet."

Ava met her gaze, the weight of her father's legacy pressing down on her. "Then we make sure we get there first."

Damian nodded, his hand resting lightly on Ava's shoulder. "We stick together. No more surprises."

Marisol hesitated, her expression softening. "For what it's worth, I'm on your side. Your father... he trusted me. I won't betray that trust."

Ava studied her for a long moment before nodding. "Let's move."

7

Chapter Seven: Echoes of the Past

The humid air of the jungle clung heavily to Ava's skin as she traced her fingers over the worn leather of her father's journal. The cryptic symbols etched into the pages pulsed with a meaning just out of reach. Beside her, Damian adjusted his bandaged arm, his expression grim yet focused. The faint crackle of a nearby campfire provided their only comfort against the encroaching darkness.

"You're too quiet," Damian said, his voice cutting through the silence. He crouched down, his steel-gray eyes searching hers. "What's on your mind?"

Ava hesitated, clutching the journal tightly. "I keep seeing him," she admitted. "My father. In my dreams, in these symbols. It's like he's guiding me, but…"

Damian reached out, his hand resting lightly on hers. "But it's not enough."

She nodded, her eyes burning with unshed tears. "He's left so much unsaid. I don't even know what I'm truly looking for anymore—the amulet, the truth, or just a piece of him."

Damian's grip tightened. "You're not alone in this, Red."

Before she could respond, the distant sound of rustling leaves snapped them both to attention. Weapons in hand, they turned toward the disturbance. Emerging from the shadows was an elder, cloaked in flowing robes, his face adorned with ceremonial paint. His dark eyes met Ava's with an intensity that froze her in place.

"You seek the Amulet of Ixchel," the elder said, his voice low and reverent. "But to find it, you must first understand the balance it represents."

The elder gestured for them to follow. Reluctantly, Ava and Damian obeyed, winding their way through the dense jungle until they reached a clearing illuminated by glowing blue fungi. The elder began to speak, recounting the legend of Ixchel's wrath and mercy—how the amulet could heal or destroy, depending on the bearer's heart.

"To wield its power," he concluded, "you must face your deepest fear."

As they followed the elder through the glowing clearing, Ava's thoughts drifted back to Elena. The sting of betrayal was fresh, and her mind churned with mistrust. She could still see Elena's sly smirk, the way she had played them, all while claiming to have their best interests at heart.

Ava's jaw tightened as Damian caught her watching him. She hated how her thoughts lingered on Elena's proximity to him during their previous encounters—the casual touches, the private conversations. It wasn't just jealousy, though that simmered beneath the surface; it was the nagging feeling that Elena knew Damian in a way Ava didn't, and that made her uneasy.

"She used us," Ava muttered, her voice low enough that only

Damian could hear.

"She used everyone," Damian replied, his tone matter-of-fact but laced with an edge. "That's how Elena works. She's a survivalist. No loyalty to anyone but herself."

Ava's fists clenched. "And yet, you seemed to trust her once."

Damian glanced at her, his steel-gray eyes unreadable in the dim light. "I didn't say I trust her now."

"Good," Ava snapped, more forcefully than she intended. "Because if she shows up again, I won't hesitate."

The tension hung between them as they approached the temple, Ava's resolve hardening. Elena's betrayal wasn't just a personal slight—it was a stark reminder of the dangers of misplaced trust. Ava promised herself she wouldn't make the same mistake again.

Trial By Shadows

Ava stood at the edge of the ancient temple, its stone steps disappearing into the darkness below. The elder's words echoed in her mind as she tightened her grip on the journal.

"Stay close," Damian said, his voice steady but low. "This place is a maze of traps."

The air inside the temple was heavy, the walls adorned with carvings depicting trials and sacrifices. The floor was lined with pressure plates, each step a potential trigger for the hidden dangers lurking in the shadows.

"Watch your step," Damian muttered as he carefully navigated the path ahead.

Suddenly, a click echoed through the corridor. Ava froze as

the walls began to shift, ancient gears grinding to life. Spears shot out from the walls, narrowly missing them. Ava's heart pounded as Damian pulled her into a small alcove.

"You okay?" he asked, his voice tense.

She nodded, her breath coming in short gasps. "This is more than a maze. It's a test."

As they moved deeper into the temple, the trials grew more personal. Ava found herself separated from Damian, standing before a room filled with shifting mirrors. Each reflection showed a version of herself—some filled with strength, others with doubt and fear. In the center of the room stood a pedestal, atop which rested a unique golden key.

A disembodied voice filled the air. "To move forward, you must embrace your truth."

Ava's reflections began to shift, each one whispering doubts and fears. "You're not enough." "You'll fail, just like your father."

"No," she whispered, her voice trembling. "I've made it this far. I'm stronger than my doubts."

She reached for the key, her hand steady despite the cacophony of whispers. As her fingers closed around it, the room went silent. The mirrors shattered, and she found herself back in the corridor, Damian has been kidnapped by the mercenaries, with the unique golden key fastened she trailed bravely behind them using their foot paths until she had a gimps of their camp.

CHAPTER SEVEN: ECHOES OF THE PAST

Ava's Infiltration of the Mercenary Camp

The night air was thick and humid as Ava crouched on a ledge overlooking the mercenary camp. Lights flickered below, casting long shadows over the makeshift structures cobbled together from tarps and corrugated metal. The hum of a generator filled the air, punctuated by the occasional burst of laughter or muffled conversation from the mercenaries patrolling the perimeter.

She scanned the camp, her heart pounding as she spotted Damian—his hands bound behind him, his face bruised but defiant. He was seated near the center of the camp, a lone figure surrounded by armed guards.

Ava's grip tightened on the knife at her side. Her father's journal was tucked safely into her pack, but its weight felt heavier than ever. This was a test, just like the elder had said. She had to prove her worth—not just to herself but to Damian, to her father's legacy, and to the mission they had set out to complete.

Sliding silently down the slope, Ava moved through the underbrush, her every step calculated to avoid detection. The jungle around her pulsed with life, the sounds of insects and distant howls masking her movements. She reached the edge of the camp, where the smell of diesel fuel and sweat mingled in the air.

Her first target was a lone guard standing near the generator. Ava crept up behind him, her knife flashing in the dim light as she disarmed him with swift precision. She dragged his unconscious body into the shadows, her breaths steady despite the adrenaline coursing through her veins.

Moving deeper into the camp, she used the cover of darkness to slip past patrols and disable key areas. A supply tent collapsed in silence after she slashed its supports, scattering the mercenaries who had been stationed nearby. Ava's movements were a blend of instinct and strategy, every action bringing her closer to Damian.

When she reached him, she knelt beside his chair, her knife slicing through his bindings with practiced ease. Damian's eyes flicked up to hers, a mix of relief and admiration shining through his exhaustion.

"Took you long enough," he murmured, his voice hoarse.

"Next time, try not to get caught," Ava shot back, a teasing edge to her tone despite the tension of the moment.

She helped him to his feet, supporting him as they slipped back into the shadows. The alarm was raised moments later, the camp erupting into chaos as mercenaries scrambled to respond to the disturbances Ava had created. Together, she and Damian disappeared into the jungle, the cacophony of shouts and gunfire fading behind them.

Tying to the Elder's Words

By the time they returned to the elder's village, the dawn light bathed the mountain city in a golden hue. The air was cooler here, the altitude bringing a crispness that was a welcome relief from the stifling humidity of the jungle. The streets were narrow and cobblestoned, lined with whitewashed buildings that gleamed in the morning sun. Brightly colored flowers spilled from windowsills, their sweet fragrance mingling with the scent of fresh bread wafting from a nearby bakery.

Ava paused in the town square, her gaze drawn to a centuries-old church standing at its center. The stone facade was weathered but proud, its bell tower rising above the surrounding rooftops. This was a place where time seemed to stand still, the echoes of history woven into every corner.

Damian leaned against a lamppost, his movements stiff but steady. "Feels almost normal here," he said, his tone contemplative.

Ava nodded, her eyes scanning the square. "This was one of my father's stops. He wrote about the city in his journal."

Damian straightened, his gaze sharpening. "Anything useful?"

"Maybe," Ava replied, pulling the journal from her pack. "He mentioned a shopkeeper who had information about Ixchel. If the man's still alive, he might know something."

They made their way through the bustling streets, the chatter of locals and the clatter of horse-drawn carts creating a vibrant symphony. Ava couldn't shake the feeling that they were being watched, though she saw no signs of pursuit. The jungle's dangers might have been left behind, but the shadow of Elliot's reach loomed large.

Chapter Eight: Beneath Amulet Chronicles

The journey to the ancient fortress was grueling, but the breathtaking Peruvian landscape offered glimpses of beauty amidst the peril. The team followed a rugged trail carved through the Andes, winding past terraced farmlands left by the Inca centuries ago. The morning mist clung to the mountains, veiling the peaks in an ethereal glow. Ava marveled at the stone structures built seamlessly into the cliffs, evidence of a civilization that understood balance and harmony with nature.

As the altitude increased, the air grew thinner, and Ava struggled to catch her breath. Damian, ever steady, adjusted his pace to match hers, offering his hand when the path grew treacherous. They reached a plateau overlooking Cusco, the historic heart of the Inca Empire, where they paused to rest. The city spread below them, its narrow cobblestone streets weaving through colonial-era buildings and bustling markets.

"This place," Ava murmured, gazing at the vibrant city, "it's alive with history."

Damian nodded, his gray eyes scanning the horizon. "And secrets. Just like us."

The temple's final chamber was vast, its ceiling lost in the darkness above. At its center stood a pedestal, and on it rested the Amulet of Ixchel. The air crackled with energy, a tangible manifestation of the artifact's power.

"There it is," Ava breathed, her voice a mix of awe and trepidation.

Before they could approach, a slow clap echoed through the chamber. Emerging from the shadows was Elliot, flanked by his mercenaries. Elena stood beside him, her expression unreadable.

"You've done well," Elliot said, his tone mocking. "Leading us right to the prize."

Damian stepped protectively in front of Ava. "You'll have to go through us to get it."

Elliot smirked. "That was always the plan."

A fierce battle erupted, the chamber becoming a battleground of clashing weapons and raw determination. Damian faced off against Elliot, their history of betrayal fueling each strike. Ava, meanwhile, confronted Elena, their fight underscored by the tension of past alliances and fresh betrayals.

"You don't have to do this," Ava said, her voice cutting through the chaos. "Help us stop him."

Elena hesitated, her blade faltering. The moment of doubt cost her; a stray mercenary's attack sent her sprawling. Ava stepped in, disarming her opponent before offering Elena a hand.

"This isn't over," Elena said, but she took Ava's hand as she ran away, the beginnings of a truce forming.

Damian tended the fire, his presence steady yet distant.

"You've been quiet," he said, breaking the silence. "You find anything yet?"

"It's not exactly a Sudoku puzzle, Cross," Ava snapped, her eyes never leaving the intricate glyphs on the stone. Her frustration wasn't just about the tablet. It was about her father. About Ixchel. About the way Damian's presence seemed to amplify every emotion she tried to suppress.

"Touchy," Damian muttered, smirking as he leaned back against a tree. "But seriously, Whitmore. What happens if this leads nowhere? If... your father's just... gone?"

The question struck a nerve. Ava's hands stilled, and for a moment, the only sound was the crackling of the fire. She looked at him, her eyes sharp and glistening.

"He's not gone," she said firmly. "I can feel it. And if this Amulet holds the answers, I'll find them."

Damian's expression softened, but he didn't push further. Instead, he nodded toward her satchel. "Just make sure that thing doesn't get us killed."

The Elliot's Insinuations

Inside the fortress, the air was thick with tension as Elliot confronted Ava and Damian. His voice was smooth, almost taunting, as he addressed Ava. "You know, Ava," he began, "your mother was quite the enigma. She had a way of... drawing people in."

Ava stiffened, her heart pounding. "Don't talk about her."

Elliot smirked, his tone deliberately provocative. "Why not? She and I had... history. Did she ever tell you about the time we spent in Lima? She was brilliant, passionate, and so utterly human in her flaws."

"You're lying," Ava spat, her fists clenched. But doubt crept in, seeded by Elliot's calculated words.

"I never lie," Elliot replied, his voice laced with condescension. "She was searching for answers, just like you. And, just like you, she trusted the wrong people."

Damian growled, stepping forward. "Enough, Elliot. If you want to settle scores, you deal with me."

Elliot's laughter echoed through the chamber, but the cracks in Ava's composure deepened. Damian placed a steadying hand on her shoulder, his presence a reminder of the truth they were fighting to uncover.

By dawn, they were on the move again. The path led them through ancient terraces and forgotten trails carved by the Inca centuries ago. Ava couldn't help but marvel at the ingenuity and beauty of the structures, though her mind remained focused on the task at hand.

"The Tears of the Sun," Ava murmured as they reached a steep staircase carved into the cliffside. "If the glyphs are correct, it's a celestial chamber. A place where... light and shadow reveal something hidden."

Damian raised an eyebrow. "A hidden something worth dying for, apparently." He gestured to the broken arrows and long-decayed remains scattered near the entrance to the chamber. "Looks like others tried to find it first."

"And failed," Ava said grimly.

Inside, the chamber opened into a vast underground hall. Rays of sunlight pierced through narrow slits in the stone, illuminating a golden altar at its center. The walls were covered in carvings depicting stories of conquest, betrayal, and the wrath of gods.

"Here," Ava whispered, stepping toward the altar. She withdrew the Amulet of Ixchel and placed it into a hollowed-out recess. As the amulet clicked into place, the room began to tremble.

"What the hell?" Damian exclaimed, drawing his weapon.

The carvings on the walls came alive with light, weaving a story that Ava deciphered in real time.

"It's a warning," she said breathlessly. "The Tears of the Sun are... not what they seem. They're..." Her voice trailed off as the light revealed a hidden passage behind the altar.

"Let me guess," Damian said. "We're going in."

Ava glanced at him, her resolve firm. "We're going in."

The passageway led to an underground cavern, its walls glimmering with crystalline formations. At the center stood a pedestal holding a golden orb, radiating a faint, warm glow.

"The Tears of the Sun," Ava said, her voice a mix of awe and trepidation.

As she approached, voices echoed through the cavern. Ava and Damian turned to see a group of armed mercenaries entering, led by a woman whose cold eyes and sharp features mirrored Ava's intensity.

"Dr. Whitmore," the woman said. "You've done all the hard work for us. Hand it over."

"Not a chance," Damian growled, stepping in front of Ava.

A tense standoff ensued, punctuated by gunfire and shouts. Ava's heart raced as she clutched the orb, its heat surging through her hands. In the chaos, she realized the orb wasn't just an artifact. It was alive.

"Ava, now would be a great time to figure out what that thing does!" Damian shouted, taking cover.

Ava closed her eyes, focusing on the orb. Images flooded her mind: her father, the amulet, the chamber, and the jungle. The orb pulsed, releasing a blinding light that sent the mercenaries fleeing succumbing to the special amulets powers.

When the light faded, the cavern was silent. Ava and Damian were alone, the orb dim but still warm in her hands.

"What just happened?" Damian asked, his voice hushed.

Ava looked at him, her expression unreadable. "I think... we've only just begun."

Elliot and Elena's Fates

Ava's determination pushed her to the pedestal holding the Amulet of Ixchel. The artifact shimmered with an otherworldly glow, its power palpable. Ignoring the chaos around her, Ava reached out, her fingers trembling as they closed around the amulet.

A sudden warmth spread through her, not just physical but emotional. Visions flooded her mind—her father's face, moments of her childhood, and the connection she'd been searching for. Tears welled in her eyes as she realized the amulet's significance went beyond her father's quest; it was a legacy of hope and renewal.

Damian, bloodied but victorious, approached her. "You did it," he said, his voice rough with emotion.

Ava turned to him, her smile radiant. "We did it."

They embraced, their bond solidified not just by survival but by shared triumph. For the first time, the weight of the journey felt lighter, and Ava allowed herself a moment of pure joy

Meanwhile, Elliot and Elena—the trusted colleagues Ava had left behind to safeguard their base camp—had their own perilous encounter. As night fell over the Peruvian jungle, a shadowy figure infiltrated their perimeter.

"Did you hear that?" Elena whispered, her hand tightening around a flashlight. The beam flickered as she scanned the dense foliage.

Elliot, more attuned to technology than survival, fumbled with his communication device. "It's probably just... an animal." But his voice betrayed his unease.

Before they could react, the intruder emerged: a mercenary scout sent by the same group hunting Ava and Damian. Chaos erupted as Elena fought to defend their supplies, her agility proving invaluable. Elliot, though terrified, managed to rig a makeshift trap using the camp's gear, incapacitating their assailant.

"We have to warn Ava," Elena said, her face pale but determined.

"And fast," Elliot agreed. They left the camp, venturing through the treacherous terrain to find Ava. Unbeknownst to them, another shadow trailed close behind, intent on finishing what the scout had started.

9

Conclusion

The Tears of the Sun had revealed more questions than answers, but Ava determination was to uncover the truth. She needs to seek answers to her past questions. She and Damian emerged from the jungle, their bond stronger than ever but tinged with unspoken tensions.

Elliot and Elena eventually reunited, battered but alive, their harrowing tale of survival adding a new layer of urgency to their mission. Together, the team vowed to stay one step ahead of those who sought to exploit the Amulet's power.

The orb's power was undeniable, and Ava knew it held the key to not only her father's disappearance but also a legacy that could reshape history.

Weeks later, Ava stood on the balcony of a modest inn overlooking the bustling streets of Cusco. The orb rested on a table beside her, its glow faint but constant.

"You're not done with this, are you?" Damian's voice came from behind her.

She turned, a small smile playing on her lips. "Not even close."

He nodded, stepping closer. "Then I guess I'm sticking around.

Someone's got to keep you out of trouble."

Ava chuckled, but her gaze drifted to the horizon. The mysteries of Ixchel and the Tears of the Sun were far from solved, and she couldn't shake the feeling that they were being watched.

Far away, in a shadowy chamber filled with maps and ancient texts, a figure studied a glowing replica of the orb. A sinister smile spread across their face.

The amulet's chamber revealed carvings that depicted not just Ixchel but elements of Andean cosmology. Ava traced the intricate symbols, recognizing depictions of Pachamama, the Earth Mother, and Inti, the Sun God. The blend of Mayan and Inca influences hinted at a deeper connection between the two ancient civilizations, a cultural exchange lost to history.

"This isn't just about one culture," Ava said, awe coloring her voice. "It's a bridge between worlds."

Damian grinned. "You're rewriting history, Whitmore."

They left the chamber, emerging into the sunlight to the sound of Quechua songs carried on the wind. The villagers below were celebrating a festival, their colorful attire and rhythmic dances paying homage to their ancestors. Ava and Damian paused, watching the celebration from afar, the amulet a symbol of hope not just for them but for the stories yet to be uncovered.

About the Author

Abiodun is an analyst by day and a storyteller by heart. With a fertile imagination and a passion for weaving intricate tales.

Beneath Amulet Chronicles: Secrets of Ava's Ixchel Adventure is his debut novel, inviting you to embark on a thrilling fantasy journey.

You can connect with me on:
- https://x.com/tpcast
- https://www.facebook.com/abiodun.thorpe